Anonymouse

Written by

Caroline Rose Kraft

Illustrated by Megan E. Cangelose

To all my pen pals around the world,
who made growing up and checking the
mailbox a delight. Also to Adalee and Eli,
who always asked about
my "next book." I love y'all.
-CRK

To my husband, who gives me courage,
to my family,
who shares my love for literature,
and to Phoebe, who was my inspiration.
-MEC

ISBN: 978-0-578-42263-3

Anonymous, *adjective*
: of unknown name.

Anonymouse, *noun*
: a mouse who wishes to remain anonymous.

POST OFFICE

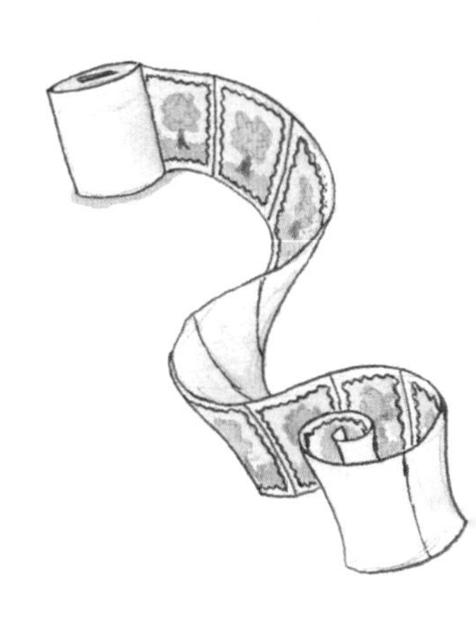

With the turn of a key, the post office was closed for the night. The old, bearded postmaster disappeared into the parking lot and bumped down the road in his dented farm truck. The stacks of stamp books sat patiently on the counter, waiting for another busy day. After a moment, the soft sound of scratching could be heard, followed by a small but definite squeak. It sounded like it was coming from P.O. Box 12. Out of all the shiny boxes, Number 12 was the last box on the top row. It had once belonged to a tall, old gentleman with a glass eye, but ever since he moved away, this box had remained empty and unclaimed...*or so the postmaster believed.*

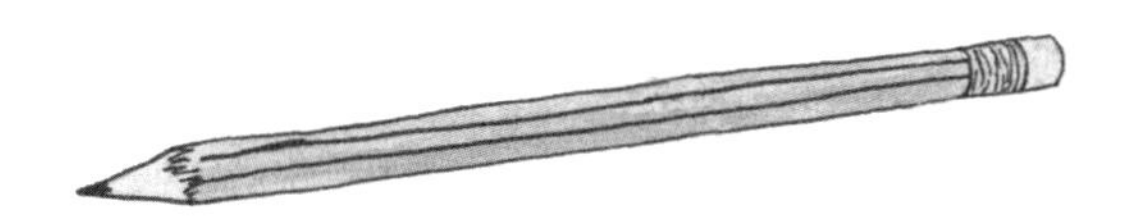

With no further warning, the door to Box 12 swung ajar. What could've made it open? It couldn't have been a gust from the air conditioning vent, nor a ghost. For gusts do not pick locks with discarded hairpins, and ghosts do not peer out into empty post offices with tentatively twitching whiskers.

Mr. Parsnip Peppersnatch was a sensible mouse who resided comfortably in P.O. Box Number 12 with his lovely wife, Coriander. Parsnip liked sweater vests, hot tea, and peace-and-quiet, which is one reason why he only opened the door once the postmaster and all the other postal workers had gone for the night. The other reason was that Parsnip was terrified. He was terrified of shoes squeaking on tile floors, sticky postage stamps, blue satchels, ink, keys, cardboard boxes, singing birthday cards, packing tape, packing peanuts, rolling bins, and credit cards. But most of all, Parsnip was terrified of people.

After several moments of peering around and sniffing, Parsnip finally scurried down the wall of tiny doors. With much caution, he scanned the post office floor, gathering crumbs and candy and such into a pile in the corner where Coriander busily pushed these findings into an envelope. Once Parsnip felt certain that he had scavenged all there was to be found, he ushered his wife back up to their small apartment, carrying the envelope in his teeth, and pulling it inside before shutting the door. Mr. and Mrs. Peppersnatch did this every night, and though Coriander longed to take the occasional stroll out in the open air, Parsnip would not stand for it.

“Too dangerous!” he would squeak. “One slip up and a whole stack of cardboard boxes could squish you flat! Too, too risky!”

Life continued this way for a long time. Some nights, Parsnip would find a whole pretzel for dinner, or a fresh rubber band for Coriander's aerobics routine. Other nights, he would mope through the door with only a few crumbs from the postmaster's lunch break. Coriander yearned for a fresh tissue to make into drapes, but again, Parsnip would twitch his whiskers and say, "Too dangerous! We can make do with the gum wrapper drapes we have now! Too, too risky!"

One afternoon, Parsnip was in their home at P.O. Box 12, trying to take a nap. Waking for the fourth time and finding that he couldn't get comfortable again, it occurred to him that the paper shreds they had stuffed their pillows with had begun to smell a bit musty and weren't as crisp as they had been a year ago. He stood up, carefully so as not to wake Coriander, and looked out the keyhole beyond the gum wrappers. The sunlight was beaming through the bustling post office. Parsnip looked down and surveyed the people racing around on their various errands. It must have been about four o'clock in the afternoon.

Oh, Parsnip thought, *look at all those shoes! Listen to them squeak on the tile floor! And all of those boxes! Probably labeled with sticky stickers and inky ink*. He shuddered a bit in his sweater (which was made of the finest toilet paper).

An old woman hobbled over to a neighboring P.O. Box, and the feather in her hat nearly tickled Parsnip's nose. A man in a hurry unlocked a box, brushed his hand through it, shut it, and dashed off again. Parsnip was about to settle back into his nest (for mice do sleep quite a bit during the day) and make another go at his nap, when the post office door opened with a jingle and something made him look back.

In the doorway stood a small girl, probably seven or eight, with a mass of corkscrew hair. She wore a blue dress, red shoes, and red ribbons around her dark pigtails; and from where Parsnip peeked, she looked very anxious. Following her was a spindly lady with a tight mouth, pointed glasses, and just the sort of loud, clomping shoes which made Parsnip quiver. The only thing the girl and the lady had in common was the dark, curly hair. The little girl wasn't smiling as she stepped toward the P.O. Boxes, holding a key as if it were a delicate flower, and scanning all of the painted numbers on the shiny little doors. After a moment, she stepped up to one of the boxes in Parsnip's view, put her key into the lock, turned it, and opened the door. She proceeded to put her whole face into the box, and when it came out again, it looked very, very sad indeed.

The little girl shut the box up again, and her brown eyes flashed up at her aunt (for that is who the lady was). She seemed unconcerned, and so the lady and the little girl walked out of the post office, leaving Parsnip to ponder. For three days in a row, the little girl came in with her aunt and checked her P.O. Box, but never was there anything inside. Each day, she seemed increasingly dejected. By the fourth day, even her ribbons seemed to droop.

47¢

On Sunday, Mr. and Mrs. Peppersnatch sat down to a dinner of cracker crumbs and a breath mint. Coriander addressed her husband. “Parsnip!” she declared. “You don’t look well at all! Whatever is troubling you, my dear?”

Parsnip, who had been resting his face on his paw, looked up with a despondent expression. “Oh, it’s just this person I keep seeing...” he muttered.

“Person?” Coriander exclaimed, dropping her utensil, which was made from a staple. “What person? Was someone here last night while you were scavenging?”

“Oh, no, no!” Parsnip frowned irritably. “Heavens, no! I’ve just seen this person from inside.”

“Well then,” Coriander huffed, stabbing another crumb. “Why are you so interested in this person?”

“I’m not sure...” Parsnip admitted, fingering his own staple. “It’s a particularly small one, for a person. And I just keep happening to see her every day. And she looks so...sad.”

Coriander found this answer very odd, but continued with her dinner nonetheless.

Early the next morning, Parsnip lay very still on his musty pillow. He felt as if he couldn't go to sleep even if he tried for a thousand mornings. And then, all of a sudden, he was up. He was at the door. He was opening it, he was crawling out, and he was gone.

The postmaster had not yet bumped up to the post office in his dented farm truck and the lights were all still unlit when Parsnip made his stealthy escape. The old Parsnip would never have dared to take a stroll so near opening hours, but something had changed in him ever since he saw that little girl with the sad, brown eyes.

When he reached the counter, he froze. He saw the ink, the boxes, and the stamps. Could he bear to go on? He glanced over his shoulder to the wall of P.O. Boxes and imagined a little girl standing there, reaching into a box to find nothing but disappointment. He wondered, for an instant, if perhaps people weren't as scary as he believed. Before he finished his thought, he found himself scampering up the leg of a chair and onto the counter. Here, he found a postcard with a painting on one side. The painting was of ballerinas in green tutus, and Parsnip decided that, though he knew nothing of young humans, this seemed like something a sad-eyed girl might enjoy.

Finding a pen, he took it in both forepaws and stood with his little feet braced against the postcard. Slowly and carefully, he wrote:

LITTLE GIRL,
WHY DO YOU LOOK SO SAD?

By this time, Parsnip was exhausted, not to mention nervous that the postmaster would arrive at any moment. He thought for a second before signing it "Anonymouse" and taking it in his teeth to deliver. However, right as he was about to slide off the counter onto the chair, something made him pause. What was missing? Ah, yes! A stamp! He scurried over to the tidy stack and found a stamp (an expensive one, just to be safe!) with a bouquet of flowers on it, and stuck it in the corner of the postcard. He even added the waves of ink over it, as he had seen on many-a-stamp.

Before going home, he used his mousy skills to open the little girl's P.O. Box and put the postcard inside. He scampered back to bed right as the lights flicked on.

The next afternoon, Parsnip was glued to the keyhole, waiting for the little girl to come. He could hardly contain his excitement! After reminding him several times that he should be in bed at this hour, Coriander demanded to know what this was all about, once and for all. Parsnip, careful not to take his gaze away from the post office floor, told his wife about last night's adventure and his mysterious postcard delivery. Poor Coriander nearly fainted.

"Who is this brave, daring mouse-man, and where has my own timid husband scurried off to?" she implored.

Finally, the little girl came in with her aunt and opened her P.O. Box. It was lucky that no one heard Mr. and Mrs. Peppersnatch as they scampered and shoved to get a good view. The aunt looked somewhat annoyed by this errand and sighed loudly. Undoubtedly, she believed there'd be no mail today, just like every day last week. The little girl looked sadder than ever, but there was some twinge of hope at the corner of her mouth as she turned the key once more.

Gingerly, she placed her small hand in the box. The little girl's eyes, which were usually quite large, grew until they were like two gold medals, gleaming at her discovery. Her aunt shut the P.O. Box and tugged her out of the post office by one hand, obviously uninterested in the invaluable treasure her niece was still clutching.

Mr. and Mrs. Peppersnatch smiled their tiny, toothy smiles at one another for a long time, quite satisfied with the scene that had just taken place.

"You have to write her again, don't you?" Coriander asked, not quite for the idea or against it.

"Not until she writes me back," Parsnip replied proudly.

The little girl came back the next day, and we can all be very glad she didn't understand how a P.O. Box works, for when she opened it, she slipped a piece of paper out of her coat sleeve and into the box before shutting it again. This, though not the traditional way to send mail, was a perfect place to leave a note to a mouse who lived just a few feet away!

That night, Parsnip snuck down while Coriander watched from above, and retrieved the letter. It was written on a large sheet of notebook paper, which had been folded many times. Unfurling it took both mice and all the space in their modest apartment. In crayon, it read:

> *Dear Anonymouse,*
>
> *I am sad because I have to stay with my aunt while my parents are away. I wish my parents would write to me so I could know when they will come and get me.*
>
> *Love,*
> *Philippa*

DEAR ANONYMOUSE,
I AM SAD
BECAUSE I
HAVE TO STAY

That night, Parsnip slinked out yet again and snatched another postcard. He wrote Philippa a short note and, a day later, he received a letter from her, this time on the back of an arithmetic sheet. They went on this way for several days, writing back and forth. The letters, both reading and writing them, were the highlight of Parsnip's nights. Even Coriander was soon quite taken with "the little dear" as they called Philippa, though she was many times their own size. Coriander cried many a mousy tear over Philippa's unfortunate circumstances, and Parsnip found new courage in everything he did for her.

Then one night, about a week and a half after the correspondence had begun, Parsnip skittered out of his P.O. Apartment to write Philippa about his favorite crayon color and some advice on steeping tea. His large handwriting had improved greatly, as had his ability to stamp postcards.

Just as he was closing Philippa's postbox again, Parsnip heard a familiar but dreaded sound behind him. Startled, Parsnip spun around, lost his grip, and nosedived to the floor. He was unharmed, but the breath was knocked out of him.

A large rolling bin, full of mail, had squeaked into view. Something beneath the heap of envelopes and packages was stirring ominously. Suddenly, as he backed toward the wall, all of Parsnip's old fears flashed through his mind.

Could it be shoes,
ready to squeak and scuff?

Could it be a postage stamp,
large enough to plaster him to the floor?

Could it be a cardboard box,
ready to swallow him up?

Could it be a bottle of ink,
about to dye him to death?

Could it be an army of keys,
picking a fight?

Could it be a singing birthday card,
springing open with some horrible dirge?

Could it be a roll of packing tape,
about to wrap him up like an adhesive mummy?

Happy Birthday
47¢

POSTAL
SERVICE

The bin trembled. Parsnip trembled. He was too frightened to face whatever he might see, but too frightened to run home. And then, quite ungracefully, a figure rose from the mess of envelopes and packages and tumbled out of the bin. It was a person, small in stature, with dark, rather messy, hair.

Parsnip couldn't believe his eyes! Philippa? What was she doing here? Yet there she was, in the same yellow dress he had seen her in this afternoon, only now very wrinkled. She stared at him as he stared at her and for several moments that was all either of them did.

Then, in a flash of instinct, Parsnip moved. While allegro music blared in his mind, he bolted at full speed, dashing hither and thither and hither again!

In an instant, he was running up a chair leg on the other side of the post office and onto the counter. He could hear Philippa's red shoes tapping on the floor behind him, and her sweet voice, for the first time. She was shouting, "Wait, wait! Don't run, Anonymouse!"

But Parsnip didn't stop to think. He ran over the counter and into the back of the post office where the postmaster sorted mail. Suddenly, he heard a thump behind him and glanced back to see Philippa, who had just climbed over the counter and landed a few feet from the very frightened mouse.

"Please," she coaxed, smoothing the yellow dress. "I'm not going to hurt you. We're friends, remember? I just wanted to meet you."

But Parsnip hadn't imagined he'd ever come so near a human, even Philippa. He couldn't even squeak. All he could do was turn around and start running again, but this time Philippa was close behind. Parsnip scurried under some bins and then under a shelf, wove through some boxes and finally dove into an open drawer. He had never been in the back of the post office before, much less in these particular drawers. The drawer he happened to jump into was full of unopened letters, and he sank down until he settled into a corner. Parsnip crouched there, breathing heavily and wondering what he had gotten himself into.

Then, all at once, the letters were being shuffled madly, and Philippa's face was an inch from Parsnip's longest whisker. Philippa gasped, and Parsnip winced. Would she grab him? Would she squeeze him? His tiny life flashed before his tiny eyes.

But to his surprise, Philippa wasn't even looking at him. Her hand reached toward him but picked up a letter instead. And then another, and another, until Parsnip was nearly entirely uncovered, yet she didn't seem to notice! It was then that Parsnip caught sight of one of the envelopes. Tilting his head sideways, he read:

"PHILIPPA"

This letter was for Philippa!
And so was this one...
and this one...
and this one!

Afterward, Parsnip never could quite tell how it happened, but suddenly he found himself in Philippa's hand, dancing with one of her fingers and squeaking for joy! Philippa was chanting, "Hooray! Hooray! Hooray! They were writing to me all along!"

The night ended with security guards flipping on the lights to find a little girl and a mouse sitting on the floor, reading a whole stack of mail together. Parsnip slipped away as Philippa explained herself (rather bravely, for a little girl) and waited for her worried aunt, who had been searching for her all evening, to come pick her up. However, little Philippa didn't mind at all. Philippa rode home with a big bag of mail in the seat next to her, thankful for her small, shy friend.

The postmaster was informed about the incident the next morning.

"Oh, bother," he muttered, tugging his beard. "I am awfully sorry about that, Miss. I suppose I am getting a little too old to manage the entire office myself, and perhaps my memory isn't as good as it once was. Now what did'ya say your name was? And which box is yours?"

Philippa told him not to think of it, and her next three letters from her parents all arrived in her postbox. The last one was a postcard, which read, "Pack your bags, Philippa! We are on our way!"

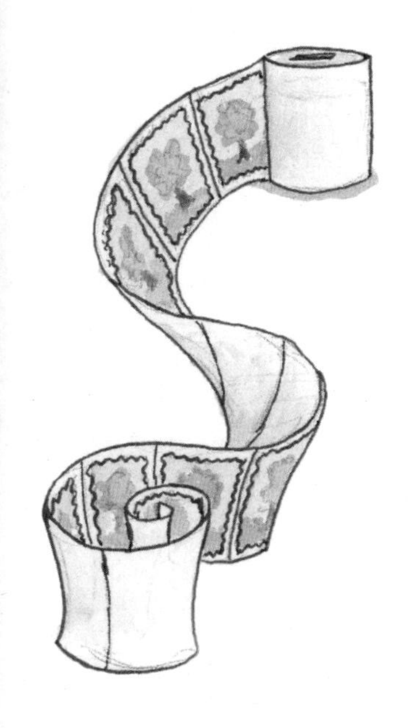

Parsnip Peppersnatch, of course, went back to living a quiet life in P.O. Box Number 12. However, he was never quite the same again. For one, Number 12 had a glorious makeover, including new drapes, much to Coriander's delight. For another, Parsnip became such a confident little critter that he introduced himself to the kindly postmaster, who, in turn, offered him a job. He now spends his nights roaming the post office, patrolling for misplaced mail. He gets paid in cheese and crackers and, of course, as many paper shreds as he could ever want.

Parsnip and Philippa remain fast friends, even now that she lives far away. For, with a little paper and ink—and some help from the postal service—friendship can span many years and many miles.

Anonymouse
Philippa

About the Author & Illustrator

CAROLINE ROSE KRAFT is a writer who never outgrew picture books. She writes them, reads them, collects them, and sometimes she even smells them. Caroline loves sunshine, chocolate, pigeons, and her two, squishy nephews. She lives with her family at a place called Eyrie Park in central Texas. *Anonymouse* is her second book.

MEGAN E. CANGELOSE is an artist with a deep love for children's literature. She has been painting since she was a little girl, and it is her artwork that brings Parsnip and company to life in *Anonymouse.* Megan lives with her darling husband and their dreamy baby, Hudson, in coastal North Carolina. *Anonymouse* is her first book.

Made in the USA
Las Vegas, NV
12 November 2022